The Mystery of the Honeybees' Secret

Elspeth Campbell Murphy

Illustrated by Joe Nordstrom

D0089417

BETHANY HOUSE PUBLISHERS
MINNEAPOLIS, MINNESOTA 55438

THREE COUSINS DETECTIVE CLUB®

9608

ELSPETH CAMPBELL MURPHY has been a familiar name in Christian publishing for over fifteen years, with more than seventy-five books to her credit and sales reaching five million worldwide. She is the author of the best-selling series *David and I Talk to God* and *The Kids From Apple Street Church*, as well as the 1990 Gold Medallion winner *Do You See Me, God?* A graduate of Trinity College and Moody Bible Institute, Elspeth and her husband, Mike, make their home in Chicago, where she writes full time.

The Mystery of the Honeybees' Secret
Copyright © 1996
Elspeth Campbell Murphy

Cover and story illustrations by Joe Nordstrom

THREE COUSINS DETECTIVE CLUB® is a registered
trademark of Elspeth Campbell Murphy.

Scripture quotation is from the Bible in Today's English Version
(*Good News Bible*). Copyright © American Bible Society 1966,
1971, 1976, 1992

Published by Bethany House Publishers
A Ministry of Bethany Fellowship, Inc.
11300 Hampshire Avenue South
Minneapolis, Minnesota 55438

Printed in the United States of America.

Library of Congress Cataloging-in-Publication Data

CIP applied for.

Contents

Kind words are like honey—
sweet to the taste and good for your health.

Proverbs 16:24

1

Fuzzy, Buzzy Little Toys

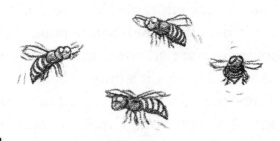

"*J*ust wait till you see them!" Sarah-Jane Cooper said to her cousins Timothy Dawson and Titus McKay, who were visiting. "They're so *adorable*! They're like little toys, you know? Little fuzzy, buzzy wind-up toys. Only, they're *alive*! And they know how to do all this neat stuff. And no one knows how they know how to do it. But it is *so cool*!"

Sarah-Jane happily took another bite of pancake coated with delicious honey.

Timothy and Titus just stared at her across the breakfast table.

Sarah-Jane had seen that look before. It meant: Our cousin has lost her mind.

She stared back at them. *"What?"*

"S-J," began Timothy. "We *are* talking about *bees*, here. Right?"

"Right," said Sarah-Jane. "So?"

"So," said Titus. "Bees sting. That doesn't sound like a very adorable thing to do."

"Don't be silly," said Sarah-Jane. "These little honeybees are so sweet they hardly sting at all. And if they do, it's only because they're defending their hives. You can't really blame them for that, can you? I've been out to the hives plenty of times, and I haven't been stung yet. We'll be all covered up in beekeeper clothes. Just don't make any sudden moves, and you'll be fine."

Timothy and Titus looked at each other doubtfully.

Sarah-Jane gave an exasperated sigh. "Look. Do you like this honey?"

"It's EX-cellent," said Titus.

"Neat-O," agreed Timothy.

"Well, where do you think it came from?" asked Sarah-Jane. "From my neighbors' very own honeybees. That's where. So if you're going to eat the honey, don't insult those darling little bees."

8

"OK, here's the deal, S-J," said Timothy. "If we agree to go out to the hives with you, you have to stop saying how cute the bees are."

Sarah-Jane thought this over. "All right," she said. "But just wait till you see them!"

2

Crabby Bees

"*A*nyway," said Sarah-Jane a little while later. "I can't wait for you to meet Mr. and Mrs. B!"

"S-J!" wailed Titus. "I thought we agreed you weren't going to talk cute about the bees."

"I wasn't!" declared Sarah-Jane indignantly.

"Oh, come on," said Timothy. "Calling the bees Mr. and Mrs.? That's pretty cute, isn't it?"

"No, no, no, no, no!" cried Sarah-Jane. "I didn't mean B-E-E. I meant just plain B. My neighbors have a long, complicated last name that no one can remember or pronounce. It starts with a B. So everyone just calls them Mr. and Mrs. B."

"Hmmm," said Titus. "Beekeepers named

Mr. and Mrs. B. That still sounds dangerously close to cute."

"They didn't do it to be cute," replied Sarah-Jane. "It just happens to be what their last name starts with. They can't help that."

She decided not to mention that Mr. and Mrs. B had also painted the mailbox at the end of their driveway to look like a giant honeybee.

"Anyway," she said. "If Mr. and Mrs. B sounds cute, it's my neighbors being cute. Not me. So I didn't break our agreement. That means you have to go out to the hives with me."

The boys knew when they were licked. And so did Sarah-Jane. She also knew that they were actually excited about seeing the bees up close.

"So," said Titus. "When do we go?"

Sarah-Jane looked up at the sky and frowned. "Not till the weather clears up. The bees don't like it when it's damp and cloudy. They can't get out into the fields the way they want to. And that makes them kind of crabby."

"Crabby bees," said Titus. "Sounds wonderful."

"Don't worry," said Sarah-Jane. "Mr. B

won't take us out to the hives until it's safe. He doesn't even go out to the hives himself in bad weather if he can help it."

"S-J!" squeaked Timothy. "I thought you said these were sweet little bees."

"They *are!*" cried Sarah-Jane. "But everybody gets crabby sometimes." She looked hard at the boys. "Especially if they're cooped up with sixty thousand whiny relatives."

"Sixty thousand?!" gasped Titus. "Did you say sixty thousand bees?"

Sarah-Jane shrugged. "Give or take a few thousand. And that's just in one hive. I can't wait for you to see them! The weatherman said it's going to get sunny this afternoon. I hope he's right."

Then Sarah-Jane thought of a way they could see the hives. Not up close. But from up high.

3

From the Attic Window

*S*arah-Jane took her cousins upstairs. Past the second floor. And on up to the attic.

Her father had recently made the attic into a big office-workroom for her mother. Sarah-Jane's mother had a decorating and sewing business. She had gotten a lot of new customers, so she needed a place to spread out her work.

The only problem was—the attic turned out to be Sarah-Jane's favorite room in the whole house, and she kept sneaking up there.

So finally her mother set up a little corner by a window just for Sarah-Jane.

The corner had its own lamp and rug and comfortable chair. It had a little bookcase and a table and chair for writing or drawing.

13

The rules were that Sarah-Jane couldn't mess with any of her mother's work stuff. And she couldn't leave her own stuff all over the place. And if her mother was working, Sarah-Jane had to be quiet and not interrupt.

So it all worked out very well. Sarah-Jane would curl up in her chair and read—mysteries mostly. Sarah-Jane loved mysteries.

So did Timothy and Titus. In fact, the three cousins had a detective club. They had solved quite a few mysteries in real life.

When Sarah-Jane wasn't reading or writing stories of her own, her favorite thing to do was just to look out of the window.

From her attic window, there was a very pretty country view of a field of wild flowers and woods beyond. But the best part was that Sarah-Jane could watch the bees.

High hedges on either side of the neighbors' yard kept the bees from bothering anybody. But from up here Sarah-Jane could look down on the hives. There were three of them. And they stood at the bottom of her neighbors' garden at the edge of the field.

She pointed them out to Timothy and Titus.

"Oh," said Titus, sounding a little disap-
pointed. "They just look like stacks of boxes."

"Almost like big, wooden filing cabinets, or
something," said Timothy.

Sarah-Jane thought about this for a minute. "They sort of look like that on the inside,
too," she said. "Except instead of pulling out

a hanging folder, you'd pull out this frame thing. And it would be covered with the honeycomb—all these little holes where the bees store the honey. And there would be bees, too, of course. Lots and lots and *lots* of bees."

Timothy and Titus glanced uneasily at each other and back at the hives. "Are you sure about this, S-J?"

"Sure, I'm sure. When it gets sunny this afternoon, a lot of the bees will go out to the field. There aren't as many flowers now as there were earlier in the summer. But the bees are still busy. The ones left in the hives are the ones who take care of the babies."

Timothy and Titus still looked a little doubtful.

Sarah-Jane said, "It's like I told you before. We'll be all covered up. Mr. and Mrs. B gave us jars of honey and beautiful beeswax candles. So, to say thank-you, my mom made them kid-sized beekeeper overalls for when their grandchildren visit. We'll be wearing those.

"And don't worry. Mr. B really knows what he's doing. Beekeeping isn't his job. He's retired, and beekeeping is his hobby. But he's very good at it. He's a very calm, careful person. Bees like that."

Suddenly Sarah-Jane sat straight up and stared out the window.

"That's odd," she said.

4

Something Odd

"What's odd?" asked Timothy and Titus together.

They crowded around the window to see what Sarah-Jane was looking at.

They saw a person coming across the field. He was wearing a full beekeeper's outfit. White overalls. Big helmet-style hat with a dark veil. Boots. Gloves.

"Isn't that just your neighbor Mr. B?" asked Timothy.

"Yes . . ." began Sarah-Jane. "I mean, no. I mean, I don't know. . . ."

Sarah-Jane bit her lip thoughtfully. "I don't know exactly. But something's wrong. Well, for one thing, I've never seen Mr. B come up to the front of the hives like that. See, each hive has just one little door for the bees to get in and out. It's in the front, facing the field. Mr. B always comes out to the hives from his house. That way he's coming up from the back, and he doesn't get in the bees' way."

Timothy said, "And didn't you say Mr. B wouldn't work on the hives when it's cloudy?"

"Yes! That, too!" cried Sarah-Jane. "He would wait till it got sunny."

"So what are you saying?" asked Titus.

Sarah-Jane shrugged. "I don't know exactly. It just doesn't look like Mr. B."

Timothy said, "But how can you tell? You can't see his face behind that dark veil. Certainly not from up here anyway."

Sarah-Jane knew that the boys weren't asking these questions to give her a hard time. They were just trying to understand what she was getting at. She tried patiently to explain.

"That person is the right height and everything. But the *attitude* is all wrong. Do you know what I mean? Mr. B has a very confident attitude. He's careful around the bees. But he's not afraid of them."

The cousins looked down at the person in the beekeeper's outfit. He had come up near the edge of the field. But he stood well back from the buzzing hives—as if wondering what to do next.

Sarah-Jane studied him a little longer.

Timothy and Titus waited patiently to hear what else she had to say.

"Here it is," said Sarah-Jane. "Something is missing that should be there. And something is there that should be missing."

"Do you want to tell us what you're talking about, S-J?" asked Timothy.

"Certainly," said Sarah-Jane. "The thing that's missing is the smoker."

Her cousins stared at her.

"Do you want to tell us what you're talking about, S-J?" asked Titus.

"Certainly," said Sarah-Jane. "A smoker is this thing that looks like a can with a spout on it. It gives off little puffs of smoke. And the smoke calms the bees down. Nobody knows exactly why that works. But it does. And Mr. B wouldn't go near the hives without it. But since he can calm the bees down like that, he doesn't usually wear gloves. That's the thing that should be missing."

Sarah-Jane could tell that her fellow detectives were impressed.

Timothy asked, "But if Mr. B doesn't wear gloves, doesn't he get stung?"

"Yes, sometimes," said Sarah-Jane. "There's really no way to keep that from happening. And some beekeepers wear gloves—especially when they're first learning how to do everything. But Mr. B thinks he can work better without them."

Titus looked out the window and said, "This guy doesn't look like he came out to work on the hives. He's just pacing back and forth."

Then, as the cousins watched, the man turned and walked back the way he had come. They lost sight of him as he went into a clump of trees.

"What's over that way?" asked Timothy.

"Just a back road," said Sarah-Jane.

As the cousins thought about this, they heard a car start up and drive away.

5

A Perfect Disguise

"What was *that* all about?" asked Timothy.

Sarah-Jane shook her head. "I have no idea."

"Do you think that guy wanted to *steal* the hives?" asked Titus.

"Could be," Sarah-Jane replied. "Hives do get stolen sometimes. But that's usually when they're far away from houses. Besides, when the hives are full of honey, they're *really* heavy. A person couldn't just pick one up and walk off with it."

"Then what was that beekeeper doing down there?" asked Timothy.

"I'm not sure he even *was* a beekeeper," said Sarah-Jane. "I mean, I'm *positive* he wasn't Mr. B. But he probably wasn't *any* bee-keeper."

"He was dressed like a beekeeper," Timothy pointed out reasonably.

"I know," said Sarah-Jane. "But somebody could be dressed up like a doctor in surgery clothes and still not know how to perform an operation. Somebody could be dressed up like a pilot. But that doesn't mean he could fly a plane."

"I see what you're saying, S-J," said Titus slowly. "This guy dresses up like a beekeeper. But he doesn't seem to know the first thing about bees. He walked across the field as if he's going to do something. But then he didn't seem to know what a beekeeper does."

"Right," said Timothy. "It was as if he just chickened out."

"Chickened out of what?" asked Sarah-Jane. "What was he doing down there?"

No one had an answer for that.

Titus said, "You know, when you think about it, a beekeeper's outfit is the perfect disguise. You're all covered up. No one can tell who you are. And if you're somewhere where there might be bees, everyone would just figure you were doing your job. No one would suspect you."

"Suspect you of what? That's the question," said Timothy. "We're right back where we started, wondering what that guy was up to."

"I don't know," said Sarah-Jane softly. "But I have a feeling he was up to no good."

6

Mr. and Mrs. B

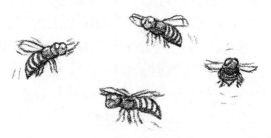

*I*t turned out that the weatherman was right. By afternoon the clouds had blown away. The day was sunny and pleasant. Not too humid. Not too hot.

"The bees don't like hot, sticky weather," Sarah-Jane said.

"Who does?" said Timothy.

Sarah-Jane ignored this. She said, "Mr. B won't try to get any work done with us kids around. He's taking us out to the hives as a favor. And it's really nice of him to do that. Beekeepers don't open the hives more than they have to. The bees don't like it when someone takes the roof off their house and a giant hand comes down and pulls them out."

"Who does?" said Titus.

"You guys be nice," said Sarah-Jane.

It was easy to be nice to Mr. and Mrs. B because they were so nice to begin with.

Mr. B wanted to make sure they weren't allergic to bee stings—just in case. They weren't.

Mrs. B helped them on with their outfits.

The overalls Sarah-Jane's mother had made were lightweight. But it still felt a little like putting on snowsuits in the summertime.

Whenever she put on the hat and veil, Sarah-Jane felt as if she were putting on a costume. She could never figure out if she felt more like a bride or a ghost or an astronaut.

"Bees don't like rough fabrics," she ex-

plained to her cousins. "And they don't like dark colors."

"Honestly!" exclaimed Titus. "These bees certainly have a lot of opinions!"

Timothy added, "And everyone says *I'm* picky!"

"You *are* picky," said Sarah-Jane and Titus together.

"Granted," said Timothy. "But at least now I know there's something in the world that's pickier than I am. Bees."

Mr. B lit the smoker, and they were off to the beeyard.

7

The T.C.D.C.

*I*n all the excitement, the cousins had almost forgotten the stranger. But now they were all dressed up like beekeepers—even though they weren't beekeepers. And that reminded them. Sarah-Jane mentioned what they had seen to Mr. B.

"He *looked* like a beekeeper," she said. "But he didn't *act* like a beekeeper. So I knew it wasn't you."

"No, it wasn't me," said Mr. B, sounding worried about it. "Mrs. B and I went shopping this morning. It was very observant of you to notice something was wrong."

"That's because we're the T.C.D.C.," said Timothy.

"What's a 'teesy-deesy'?" asked Mr. B.

"It's letters," explained Sarah-Jane. "Capital T. Capital C. Capital D. Capital C. It stands for the Three Cousins Detective Club."

"Detectives, eh?" said Mr. B. "I like mysteries myself. But I don't like the idea of someone prowling around my beehives. You sure he didn't touch anything?"

"He didn't go near the hives," said Timothy. "He just stood there looking at them."

"Hmmm," said Mr. B. "Who was he, I wonder? And what did he want?"

The cousins wished they had answers for those questions.

They looked up at the attic window. It was funny to think that a little while ago they had been up there, looking down on the hives. And now they were down by the hives, looking up at the window.

"We can keep an eye out for you, Mr. B," Sarah-Jane offered. "If we see anything odd again, we'll call you and let you know."

Mr. B smiled. "I appreciate that! It will be like having my own Sherlock Holmes living right next door."

Titus, who loved the Sherlock Holmes stories his father read him, suddenly remembered something interesting.

He said, "Hey, you know what? When Sherlock Holmes retired from being a great detective, you know what he did? He moved to the country and raised bees!"

"That's right! He did!" exclaimed Mr. B. "Well, now. It looks like we all have two things in common. We all love mysteries. And we all love bees."

"Tim and Ti aren't sure they love bees," said Sarah-Jane.

"Hmmm," laughed Mr. B. "We'll just have to convince them, won't we, Sarah-Jane?"

Inside the Hive

*M*r. B aimed a puff of smoke at the entrance to the hive down near the ground. Then he took the top off the hive and gave a couple more puffs there.

When the bees were calm, he pulled out one of the hanging frames and showed it to the cousins.

Timothy and Titus forgot all about being nervous, Sarah-Jane noticed.

Mr. B explained what the bees were doing and how the hive worked.

"Neat-O!" whispered Timothy.

"EX-cellent!" agreed Titus.

Sarah-Jane and Mr. B looked at each other and smiled.

Mr. B said, "The bees gather nectar from

the flowers and turn it into honey for their food. But they make lots more than they need. So beekeepers gather the extra as food for people. But, for me, honey is just an excuse to keep bees. I love bees! I know they're just little insects. But I treat them gently with kind words and thoughts."

"Do they like that?" said Timothy.

"Who knows? They seem to," Mr. B said with a smile as he carefully closed up the hive.

"Where did you get the bees?" asked Titus. "Did you capture them from a hollow tree or something?"

Before Mr. B could answer, Sarah-Jane said, "That's one way to get bees. But Mr. B just ordered a few pounds of bees through the mail."

Timothy and Titus stared at her. It was the our-cousin-has-lost-her-mind look. Sarah-Jane had a reputation in the family for her vivid imagination. And she had been known to exaggerate. . . .

Mr. B came to her rescue. "It's true," he said, laughing at the looks on the boys' faces. "A group of bees is called a colony. And their home is called a hive. I started this hive with a packet of bees. There's one queen in the hive, and she's the only one that lays eggs for baby bees. But she lays thousands and thousands and thousands. So my colony grew well."

He pointed to the other two hives, and his smile grew a little sad.

"These hives belonged to a very dear friend of mine. One hive is full and the other is empty. My friend was hoping to expand. So now I'll do that for him. He died not too long ago. His wife wasn't able to do the work, and his sons don't know much about bees. So my friend asked his wife to give the bees to me."

Sarah-Jane nodded, as if thinking of a sad but beautiful story. She said, "And when your friend died, you and his wife and Mrs. B went out to tell the bees."

9

Telling the Bees

*T*imothy and Titus were staring at her again. Really, this was getting kind of tiresome.

Sarah-Jane stared back at them. *"What?"*

Titus said, "S-J, please!"

Timothy said, "Telling the bees?"

Mr. B came to her rescue again. He said, "People have kept bees for thousands of years. But it's only recently that we've begun understanding how they do their work. Long ago, people believed things about bees that aren't true. But it's something like a folk tale, something kind of nice to think about. One of those beliefs was that if the beekeeper died, someone had to go out and tell the bees. Otherwise the bees would die, too—or all fly away.

"So when my friend died, some of us gathered at his hives. We told the bees what had happened and that I would be the new bee-keeper. It sounds a little silly, but it wasn't at all. It was like a little memorial service, and it was really very sweet."

Sarah-Jane said, "People used to think they were supposed to tell the bees whenever anything important happened."

She repeated a little rhyme that Mrs. B had taught her:

> *Marriage, birth or burying,*
> *News across the sea,*
> *All your sad or merrying*
> *You must tell the bees.*

Mr. B added, "And people used to believe that bees couldn't do well in a family where people fought and didn't get along."

"That one makes sense to me," said Titus. "Because you have to be calm around the bees. And if people are stomping around and yelling, the bees are going to get upset, too. Right?"

"Absolutely," said Mr. B. "Bees need to be treated with gentleness and kindness. So do people, come to think of it!

"Unfortunately, my friend's sons didn't get along. Not when they were boys and not even now when they're all grown up.

"It was always my friend's dream to go into business with his sons. He had a secret recipe for honey syrup that had been passed down from his great-grandmother. He thought if he could market it, he would have a good little business. And he would have, too, if his sons could only get along."

"Which son got the recipe?" asked Titus.

"Neither one, as far as I know," said Mr. B. "My friend always said he would give it to me to keep for them when they were ready to work together. But he never did. And his wife has never seen it."

They had all wandered out to the field to see if they could watch a bee gathering nectar from a flower. But sometimes, when you're looking for one thing, you find something else. The cousins were looking for bees. And they found some.

But that's not all they found.

10

A Clue in the Field

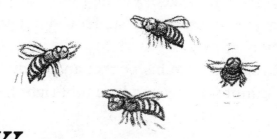

"What is it?" asked Timothy, picking it up. Sarah-Jane took off her veil to get a better look.

Timothy and Titus did the same when Sarah-Jane explained that they didn't need to wear them away from the hives. She didn't think she had to explain that she kept hers on longer than she had to because it made her feel dramatic and mysterious. Fortunately, the boys didn't ask about that. They were too interested in what Timothy held in his hand.

"It's a tool of some kind," said Timothy. "It looks like a crowbar, but a lot smaller."

"Looks familiar," said Titus. "I saw something like it not too long ago."

"Of course you did," said Sarah-Jane. "That's because it's Mr. B's hive tool. He used it to open the hives." She called to Mr. B who was puttering around the hives. "Mr. B! You dropped this!"

"Did I?" he asked, coming over to them. "I'll have to be more careful. How did it get all the way over here?"

He reached into his pocket and said, "No, wait a minute. I have my hive tool right here."

"Maybe this is your extra one," said Sarah-Jane.

"No," said Mr. B. "I keep that one in the toolbox in my house. It's a handy little gadget. I used it only this morning to pry open a sticky drawer."

Sarah-Jane began to feel uneasy.

She said what they were all thinking. "Well, if this isn't yours, whose is it? And what's it doing here?"

The cousins looked at one another as if they were all remembering the same thing at the same time.

"You know—" began Timothy slowly. "We're standing right about where that guy was this morning. . . ."

Titus said, "That doesn't mean he dropped it, but I have a bad feeling about this."

"So do I," said Sarah-Jane.

"But what does it mean?" asked Mr. B. "That someone was planning to pry open my hives? Why?"

11

Questions

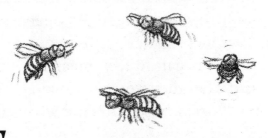

"*T*o steal honey?" asked Titus. "Is that why someone would break into a hive?"

"Possibly," replied Mr. B. "I've heard of that happening. But I've already collected the last of the extra honey for this year. The busiest honey-making time is over for the bees. It might feel like a warm summer's day. But it's time for the bees to start winding down for winter."

Timothy said, "Besides. Breaking into a hive seems like a lot of trouble to go to just to get some honey. How much honey does a person need, anyway? And you can just buy it from the beekeeper or a store."

There was a question Sarah-Jane didn't want to ask. But she felt she had to face it. She said, "Mr. B—you don't think that guy was just here to *wreck* the hives, do you? You know . . . like vandalism?"

"Vandalism!" cried Timothy and Titus together.

Mr. B shook his head sadly. "It can be a real problem with beehives. People tip them over or throw rocks at them."

"That's—that's *outrageous!*" sputtered Timothy. "Here you have these sweet little bees just trying to do their work and some creep comes along and tries to hurt them. For no reason!"

"It's terrible!" agreed Titus hotly. "Poor little bees! They never hurt anyone. They don't even sting unless they're defending their hive. And you can't blame them for that. So why can't people just leave them alone?"

Sarah-Jane bit the inside of her cheek to keep from laughing. The idea of vandalism certainly wasn't funny. But she never thought she'd hear Timothy and Titus talking about the poor, sweet little bees. Not after the hard time they had given her at breakfast for "talking cute" about the bees.

Mr. B said, "Vandalism is an awful thing. I

totally agree with you. But I don't think that is what's going on here. Not from what you've told me you saw. The idea of someone dressing up in a beekeeper's outfit and just looking at the hives . . . Vandalism is more spur-of-the-moment than that. And it usually happens when hives are off by themselves somewhere. Not in someone's yard. No, I think something else is going on here. I only wish I knew what it was."

The cousins looked at one another. They were detectives, weren't they? And they were going to get to the bottom of this.

Somehow.

12

A Sticky Situation

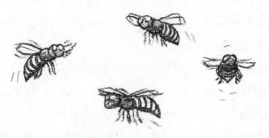

*T*he cousins followed Mr. B to the work shed at the back of the house. There they all hung up their outfits.

Then Mr. B got down a battered old notebook and jotted something in it.

He explained, "I keep a record of every time I open the hive or do some work on it," he explained. "The other notebook belonged to my friend. When I work on the other hive, I make a note in it. It probably would make sense to put all the notes in one notebook. But I keep up the one that belonged to him."

They went into the kitchen, and Mr. B showed them the machine he used for spinning the honey out of the comb. That way the empty comb could be used again by the bees.

"It's sticky work!" said Mrs. B. "But it's well worth it."

She gave Timothy and Titus jars of honey to take home. (Sarah-Jane already had plenty.)

Mr. and Mrs. B had to be gone for the rest of the afternoon.

"Don't worry," Sarah-Jane told Mr. B as the cousins said thank-you and left to go back home. "We'll keep an eye on the bees. We'll let you know if anything else unusual happens."

When they were back home, the cousins tried to decide what to do next.

Timothy and Titus thought they should go back to the field to look for clues.

Sarah-Jane thought they should go back to the attic room to keep a lookout.

They figured they could do both without fighting about it. So they picked a time to meet up and compare notes. Then the boys went looking for clues. And Sarah-Jane went up to her attic window.

From up there she could see her cousins clearly. They were walking slowly, looking down. Sarah-Jane saw a man walking toward them before the boys did. He had come from the direction of the back road. He was not

wearing beekeeper clothes.

The man came up to Timothy and Titus. From the way he was pointing, it looked as if he were asking them directions.

Timothy and Titus didn't seem to be saying much. They just kept shaking their heads and shrugging.

Finally, the man turned and went back the way he had come.

When he was safely out of sight, Timothy and Titus turned and looked up at the window.

From the expressions on their faces, Sarah-Jane could tell something was up.

She ran downstairs to meet them.

"What was that all about?" she asked.

"You are not going to believe this!" said Timothy. "He was asking about Mr. B. He wanted to know if this was where he lived and if those were his hives."

"What did you tell him?" gasped Sarah-Jane.

"Nothing," said Titus. "And we didn't lie and say we didn't know Mr. B, either. We just kept saying, 'We don't live here. We're just visiting.' Which is the absolute truth."

The cousins had found something out in their experience as detectives. And that was—sometimes if you just kept quiet, the other person would just keep talking. If that other person was up to something, it was a good way to find out.

"What was he doing there?" asked Sarah-Jane.

Titus said, "That's just it. It was as if he felt he had to explain to us what he was doing there. I mean, what do we care? We're just a couple of kids playing in the field, right? But he says he's looking for Mr. B to check his bee-keeping records, that he has to see his note-book."

"And then he told us the most ridiculous lie!" said Timothy. "S-J, you are not going to believe what he told us. He said he was—get this—the *bee inspector*! I mean, is that crazy, or what?"

"It most certainly is!" snorted Sarah-Jane. "I happen to know the bee inspector. And it's *not him*."

13

The Bee Inspector

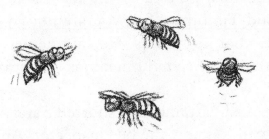

Sarah-Jane's cousins were staring at her. And they had "that look" on their faces again. Really, this had to stop.

"*What?*" she yelled.

"Oh, come on, S-J" said Timothy, laughing. "You don't really expect us to believe that there's such a person as the bee inspector, do you?"

"Sure, I do. He goes to my church."

"The bee inspector goes to your church," repeated Titus.

"That's what I said," replied Sarah-Jane.

"Ohh, Kaayy," said Timothy slowly. "What does the bee inspector do?"

"What do you think he does?" cried Sarah-Jane. "He *inspects bees*! It's the law. Bees can get

48

sick just like anyone else. The bee inspector
has to check to make sure there's no disease
that can spread."

"Oh," said Timothy, knowing when he was
licked. "That makes sense, I guess."

"So you're saying this guy is legit?" asked
Titus.

"No," said Sarah-Jane. "Because I think
there's only one bee inspector for this area.
And even if this guy were an assistant or something, he wouldn't come out alone. He would
make an appointment, and the beekeeper
would go with him. Mr. B wouldn't have gone
away for the afternoon if the inspector were
coming."

"Then who is this guy?" asked Titus.

"That's what *I'd* like to know," said Sarah-
Jane. "Do you think he's the same guy we saw
this morning?"

Timothy said, "I can't be sure, of course,
but my guess would be no. I'm pretty sure the
other guy was taller."

"Me, too, now that you mention it," said
Titus.

"So what do we do now?" asked Timothy.

"We'll tell Mr. B as soon as he gets back, of course. . . ."

They were all feeling kind of helpless. Two strangers asking about the beehives. What was going on?

Suddenly Sarah-Jane had an idea. "I know something we can do. The second guy asked about the notebooks. Well, what if he comes back? The work shed isn't locked. Maybe we should get the notebooks and keep them in a safe place until Mr. B gets back."

"Good thinking, S-J!" said Timothy and Titus.

First the cousins ran upstairs to the attic to take a good look around. The coast was clear. Then they slipped out the back door. They still looked around to make sure they weren't being spotted. Then they slipped over to the work shed as carefully as spies. They were really pretty good at that sort of thing.

The notebooks were still where Mr. B had left them.

Sarah-Jane took them down and slipped them into her pockets.

Timothy said, "But what if Mr. B comes back to get the notebooks before we get a chance to tell him where they are?"

"We could leave him a note," said Titus.

"Good idea," said Sarah-Jane.

She tore a blank page out of the back and wrote:

> *Dear Mr. B,*
> *We are keeping the notebooks safe.*
> *Sincerely, S-J C., T.D., T. M.*

"Now where do we leave our note so that Mr. B will find it but the strangers won't?" asked Timothy.

"I have an idea," said Sarah-Jane.

14

The Beekeeper's Notebook

Sarah-Jane led her cousins past the house and down the long driveway to the edge of the road.

"Oh, look!" said Titus. "Mr. and Mrs. B painted their mailbox to look like a honeybee! That's really cute!"

"It's very artistic," agreed Timothy. "I love it!"

Sarah-Jane put these comments on her mental list of things she thought she'd never hear in a million years.

Mr. and Mrs. B had already gotten their mail, so the flag was down.

Sarah-Jane put the note in the box and put the flag up again.

That way, when Mr. and Mrs. B came back to the driveway, they would be curious and look inside. But a stranger would just think they hadn't gotten their mail yet.

That done, Sarah-Jane said, "I wonder what's so important about these notebooks? Mr. B showed me how he keeps track of the work he does on the hives. He even let me write in it one day when I helped him."

Since Sarah-Jane had already seen inside

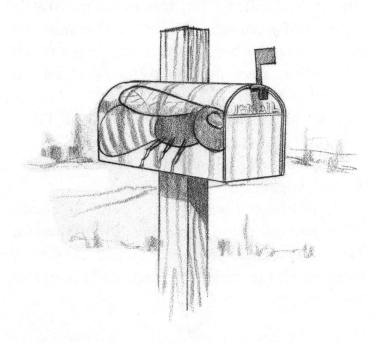

the notebooks with Mr. B there, the cousins figured it would be all right to look through them again now.

They decided to take the notebooks up to Sarah-Jane's corner in the attic room. That way, they could watch from the window to see when Mr. B got back. They were dying to tell him about the latest odd thing—another visitor to the hives. And they could also keep an eye on the hives to see if anything else happened.

They looked through Mr. B's notebook first. It was filled with neat printing. Mostly dates and numbers. There were comments about how the bees were doing. How much honey they were making. What work Mr. B had done when.

"What are we looking for?" asked Titus. "This all seems pretty ordinary to me."

"Maybe the numbers are codes or something," suggested Timothy.

The cousins were pretty good at codes. They had even made up a few of their own for sending messages to one another. And they were careful to make sure their code books all matched.

They knew that sometimes you could crack a code if you looked for something unusual. Something that stood out from the other things around it. Figuring out what that thing meant was sometimes the key that unlocked the rest.

They went back through Mr. B's notebook again. Nothing.

They decided to set it aside for a while and look at the notebook that belonged to Mr. B's friend.

The latest notes were in Mr. B's own neat printing from when he had taken over the hive.

The first part of the notebook was also dates and notes about bees, bees, bees.

Nothing jumped out at them at first.

And then it did.

At first it just looked like a bunch of numbers in among all the other numbers. But it wasn't pounds of honey. And it wasn't a calendar date. It was a string of numbers. But some of them had *R* in front of them. And some of them had *L*.

"*R* for right," said Timothy.

"*L* for left," said Titus.

"The combination to a safe," said Sarah-Jane.

They wouldn't even have noticed the page at all if Mr. B's friend hadn't doodled on it. A little swarm of honeybees. And it was only by looking very, very closely that the cousins saw that each little bee had a letter on its side. And the letters put together spelled the word *strongbox*.

The cousins had been thinking so hard that they jumped about a mile straight up when Sarah-Jane's mother came in.

"Mr. B is here to see you kids," she said. "Something about notebooks?"

The cousins practically flew downstairs.

It took a while—quite a while—to explain to Mr. B what they had found.

"I never noticed that before!" he said. "Do you know what I think this is? I think this is where my friend hid his old secret family recipe. In the strongbox. But he never gave it to me."

Titus said, "What good is the combination without the strongbox?"

Timothy added, "And what good is the strongbox without the combination? The two

56

things have to go together."

Mr. B said, "And why didn't my friend tell anyone what he was doing?"

Sarah-Jane was quiet, thinking hard.

"Maybe he did," she said softly. "Maybe he told the bees."

15

The Empty Hive

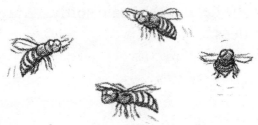

"*A*nd don't you dare look at me funny!" Sarah-Jane yelled at her cousins before they could do any such thing. "It just so happens I have thought of a perfect hiding place. A place that looks very ordinary. But where there are thousands and thousands and thousands of guards."

"A beehive?" asked Timothy and Titus together.

"The empty beehive!" cried Mr. B. "Of course! My friend knew I would have to take it apart either this fall or next spring. He knew I would find the strongbox sooner or later. If that's indeed where it is."

They were all just about to rush out to put on their beekeeper outfits when Mrs. B came

out her back door. With her were two embar-
rassed-looking young men.

"My friend's sons," Mr. B murmured to
the cousins. "I wonder what they've been up
to now?"

The older one, whose name was Mark,
spoke first. "Our dad wrote letters to us before
he died. He gave them to his lawyer to keep for
a while. Then the lawyer was to send them to
us. We both just got them."

The younger son, whose name was James,
said, "I think we'd better read them to you."

Mark went first. He got all choked up, but
he was able to get through it.

My dear son, Mark,
  I always loved you best. That's why I'm
telling you that the secret recipe is hidden in
a strongbox in the empty hive. Don't try to
get it alone. Ask Mr. B to help you.
  Love, Dad.

The cousins didn't want to interrupt. But
when they heard the part about the empty
hive, they couldn't help grinning and punch-
ing one another.

Mark said, "But I didn't want to get help

from Mr. B, because I knew he would want me to share the recipe with my brother."

Titus said, "So you dressed up in a bee-keeper's outfit and thought you could open the hives by yourself. But you gave up."

Mark looked at him in surprise. "How did you know that?"

James looked at Timothy and Titus closely. "Hey, aren't you the kids I talked to earlier this afternoon? The ones who said they don't live here?"

Timothy shrugged. "Hey, don't look at *us*. We're just visiting. But what about you? You were looking for the notebook, weren't you?"

James nodded and read his father's letter:

My dear son, James,

I always loved you best. That is why I'm telling you that the combination to the strongbox is written in my beekeeper's note-book. In the strongbox you will find the secret recipe. Don't try to get it alone. Ask Mr. B to help you.

Love, Dad.

Sarah-Jane said, "Don't tell me. Let me guess. You didn't want to get help from Mr. B, because you knew he would want you to share the recipe with your brother."

James nodded.

Mr. B said, "But the fact that you gentlemen are here together is a good sign. Neither one of you could get the recipe alone. Does this mean that you're willing to work together?"

Mark and James looked at each other and smiled.

"Yes, sir, it does," said Mark.

"We got together and talked some things out," agreed James. "We're definitely on the right track."

"Glad to hear it," said Mr. B. "Because you can come with me to get the strongbox out of the empty hive if you want. But only kind words and gentle thoughts around my little bees."

"Thank you very much, sir," said Mark. "But I'd rather wait here. I've had enough of bees for one day."

"That's something else we agree on," said James.

"Very well," said Mr. B. "My young friends will come with me."

So, for the second time that day, the cousins got dressed up in their beekeeper outfits and headed out to the hives.

The strongbox was hidden in the empty hive. Just where Sarah-Jane had guessed it might be.

All around them the bees flew back and forth to the hives. Sarah-Jane couldn't help murmuring, "Oh, you're just so adorable,

aren't you? You're just like fuzzy, buzzy little wind-up toys."

But she must have spoken louder than she had meant to, because Timothy and Titus were staring at her.

Sarah-Jane stared back at them. *"What?"*

The End

Series for Young Readers*
From Bethany House Publishers

★　★　★

BACKPACK MYSTERIES
by Mary Carpenter Reid

This excitement-filled mystery series follows the mishaps and adventures of Steff and Paulie Larson as they strive to help often-eccentric relatives crack their toughest cases.

★　★　★

THE CUL-DE-SAC KIDS
by Beverly Lewis

Each story in this lighthearted series features the hilarious antics and predicaments of nine endearing boys and girls who live on Blossom Hill Lane.

★　★　★

RUBY SLIPPERS SCHOOL
by Stacy Towle Morgan

Join the fun as home-schoolers Hope and Annie Brown visit fascinating countries and meet inspiring Christians from around the world!

★　★　★

THE THREE COUSINS DETECTIVE CLUB®
by Elspeth Campbell Murphy

Famous detective cousins Timothy, Titus, and Sarah-Jane learn compelling Scripture-based truths while finding—and solving—intriguing mysteries.

* (ages 7–10)